Scary Fairy Tales

Jack the Giant Killer

and other stories

Compiled by Vic Parker

Miles Kelly

First published in 2012 by Miles Kelly Publishing Ltd
Harding's Barn, Bardfield End Green, Thaxted, Essex, CM6 3PX, UK

2 4 6 8 10 9 7 5 3 1

Publishing Director Belinda Gallagher
Creative Director Jo Cowan
Editor Sarah Parkin
Designer Jo Cowan
Editorial Assistants Lauren White, Amy Johnson
Production Manager Elizabeth Collins
Reprographics Stephan Davis, Jennifer Hunt, Thom Allaway

ISBN 978-1-84810-589-8

Printed in China

British Library Cataloguing-in-Publication Data
A catalogue record for this book is available from the British Library

ACKNOWLEDGEMENTS
The publishers would like to thank the following artists who have contributed to this book:
Cover: Gerald Kelley at The Bright Agency
Advocate Art: Luke Finlayson
The Bright Agency: Si Clark, Peter Cottrill, Gerald Kelley
Duncan Smith
All other artwork from the Miles Kelly Artwork Bank

The publishers would like to thank the following sources for the use of their photographs:
iStockphoto.com, Shutterstock.com (cover) donatas1205, Eky Studio; (page decorations) alarik,
dmiskv, Ensuper, Eugene Ivanov, Ints Vikmanis, mariait

Every effort has been made to acknowledge the source and copyright holder of each picture.
Miles Kelly Publishing apologises for any unintentional errors or omissions.

Made with paper from a sustainable forest

www.mileskelly.net   info@mileskelly.net

www.factsforprojects.com

CONTENTS

The Third Voyage of Sinbad the Sailor

An extract from *The Arabian Nights Entertainments*,
retold by Andrew Lang

Long ago, a Middle Eastern man called Sinbad went to sea to seek his fortune in strange lands. On his first voyage, he landed on what appeared to be an island but was an enormous, sleeping whale! When the whale dived, Sinbad was washed ashore on another island. Here, he helped to save a king's horse from drowning. The king rewarded Sinbad richly and he returned to Baghdad wealthy. Soon restless, Sinbad set off on a second voyage. Once accidentally abandoned by his shipmates, he found himself stranded in a valley of diamonds. He was lifted out of the valley by a gigantic bird called a roc, and returned to Baghdad with a fortune in gems.

AFTER A VERY SHORT TIME the pleasant, easy life I led made me quite forget the perils of my two voyages. So once more I set sail with other merchants of my acquaintance for distant lands. One day upon the open sea we were caught by a terrible wind. It drove us into harbour on a strange island.

"I would rather have come to anchor anywhere than here," exclaimed our captain. "This island is inhabited by hairy savages. Whatever these dwarfs may do we dare not resist, since they swarm like locusts, and if one of them is killed the rest will fall upon us, and speedily make an end of us."

Only too soon we were to find out that the captain spoke truly. There appeared a vast multitude of hideous savages, covered with reddish fur. Throwing themselves into the waves, they surrounded our vessel. They swarmed up the ship's side with such speed and agility that they almost seemed to fly.

They sailed our vessel to an island which lay a little further off, where they drove us ashore; then they made off with our ship, leaving us helpless.

We wandered miserably inland. Presently we saw in the distance what seemed to us to be a splendid palace, towards which we turned our weary steps. But when we reached it we saw that it was a castle. Pushing back the heavy, ebony doors we entered the courtyard, but upon the threshold of the great hall beyond it we paused, frozen with horror, at the sight which greeted us. On one side lay a huge pile of bones – human bones, and on the other numberless spits for roasting! Overcome with terror, we sank trembling to the ground and lay there in despair.

A loud noise aroused us. The door of the hall was burst open and a horrible giant entered. He was as tall as a palm tree and had one eye, which flamed like a burning coal in the middle of his forehead. His teeth were long and sharp, while his lower lip hung down upon his chest. He had ears like an elephant's ears, and nails like the claws of some fierce bird.

The giant examined us with his fearful eye, then came towards us, and grabbed me by the back of the neck, turning me this way and that. Feeling that I

was mere skin and bone he set me down again and went on to the next, whom he treated in the same fashion; at last he came to the captain, and finding him the fattest, he stuck him upon a spit and kindled a huge fire at which he roasted him. After the giant had supped he lay down to sleep, snoring like the loudest thunder, while we lay shivering with horror the whole night through.

When day broke he awoke and went out. Then we bemoaned our horrible fate, until the hall echoed with our despairing cries. Though we were many and our enemy was alone, no plan could we devise to escape from the island. So at last, submitting to our sad fate, we spent the day in wandering up and down the island eating what we could find. When night came we returned to the castle, having sought in vain for any other place of shelter.

At sunset the giant returned, supped upon one of our unhappy comrades, slept and snored till dawn, and then left us as before. Our condition seemed to us so frightful that several of my companions thought it would be better to leap from the cliffs and perish in the waves at once, rather than await so miserable an end; but at last I had an idea to combat the giant. I told it to my companions, then added, "Plenty of driftwood lies along the shore. Let us make several rafts. If our plot succeeds, we can wait patiently for some passing ship to rescue us. If it fails, we must quickly take to our rafts; frail as they are, we have more chance of saving our lives with them than we have if we remain here."

All agreed with me, and we spent the day building rafts, each capable of carrying three persons. At nightfall we returned to the castle, and very soon in came the giant, and one more of our number was sacrificed. But the time of our vengeance was at hand! As soon as he had finished his horrible repast he lay down to sleep as before, and when we heard him begin to snore I, and nine of the boldest of my comrades, rose softly and took a spit, which we made red-hot in the fire. Then at a given signal we plunged it into the giant's eye, completely blinding him.

Uttering a terrible cry, he sprang to his feet clutching in all directions to try to seize one of us, but we had all fled different ways as soon as the deed was done, and thrown ourselves flat upon the ground in corners where he was not likely to touch us.

After a vain search he fumbled about till he found the door, and fled out of it howling frightfully. We too fled from the castle and, stationing ourselves beside our rafts, we waited to see what would happen.

Alas! Morning light showed our enemy approaching us, supported on either hand by two giants nearly as large and fearful as himself. Hesitating no longer we clambered upon our rafts and rowed with all our might out to sea. The giants seized up huge pieces of rock and, wading into the water, hurled them after us with such good aim that all the rafts except the one I was upon were swamped, and their luckless crews drowned. Indeed I and my two companions had all we could do to keep our own raft beyond the reach of the giants. But by dint of hard rowing we at last gained the open sea.

Jorinda and Jorindel

By the Brothers Grimm

THERE WAS ONCE an old castle that stood in the middle of a deep, gloomy wood, and in the castle lived an old fairy. Now this fairy could take any shape she pleased. All day long she flew about in the form of an owl, or crept about like a cat; but at night she always became an old woman again. When any young man came within a hundred paces of her castle, he became quite fixed, and could not move a step till she came and set him free; but when any pretty maiden came within that space she was changed into a bird, and the fairy put her into a cage, and hung her up in a chamber in the castle. There were seven hundred of these cages hanging in the castle, and all with beautiful birds in them.

Now there was once a maiden whose name was Jorinda. She was prettier than all the pretty girls that ever were seen before, and a shepherd lad, whose name was Jorindel, was very fond of her, and they were soon to be married. One day they went to walk in the wood, that they might be alone; and Jorindel said, "We must take care that we don't go too near to the fairy's castle."

It was a beautiful evening; the last rays of the setting sun shone bright through the long stems of the trees upon the green underwood beneath, and the turtle-doves sang from the tall birches. Jorinda sat down to gaze upon the sun; Jorindel sat by her side; and both felt sad, they knew not why; but it seemed as if they were to be parted from one another for ever. They had wandered a long way; and when they looked to see which way they should go home, they found themselves at a loss to know what path to take.

The sun was setting fast. Jorindel on a sudden looked behind him, and saw through the bushes that they had, without knowing it, sat down close under the old walls of the castle. Then he shrank for fear, turned pale, and trembled.

Jorinda was just singing, when her song stopped suddenly. Jorindel turned to see the reason, and beheld his Jorinda changed into a nightingale! Jorindel could not move; he stood fixed as a stone, and could neither weep, nor speak, nor stir hand or foot.

And now the sun went quite down; the gloomy night came;

14

and the old fairy came forth pale and meagre, with staring eyes, and a nose and chin that almost met one another. She mumbled something to herself, seized the nightingale, and went away with it in her hand.

Poor Jorindel saw the nightingale was gone — but what could he do? He could not speak, he could not move from the spot where he stood. At last the fairy came back and on a sudden Jorindel found himself free. Then he fell on his knees before the fairy, and prayed her to give him back his dear Jorinda: but she laughed at him, and said he would never see her again; then she went her way.

He prayed, he wept, he sorrowed, but all in vain. "Alas!" he said. "What will become of me?" He could not go back to his own home, so he went to a nearby village, and employed himself in keeping sheep. Many a time did he walk round and round as near to the hated castle as he dared go, but all in vain; he heard or saw nothing of Jorinda.

At last he dreamed one night that he found a beautiful purple flower, and that in the middle of it lay a costly pearl; and he dreamed that he plucked the flower, and went with it in his hand into the castle, and that everything he touched with it was disenchanted, and that there he found his Jorinda.

In the morning when he awoke, he began to search over hill and dale for this pretty flower; and eight long days he sought for it in vain: but on the ninth day, early in the morning, he found the beautiful purple flower; and in the middle of it was a large dewdrop, as big as a costly pearl. Then he plucked the flower, and travelled day and night, till he came again to the castle. He walked nearer than a hundred paces to it, and yet he did not become fixed as before, but found that he could go quite close up to the door. Jorindel was very glad indeed to see this. Then he touched the door with the flower, and it sprang open; so that he went in through the court and listened, hearing many birds singing.

At last he came to the chamber where the fairy sat, with the seven hundred birds singing in the seven hundred cages. When the fairy saw Jorindel she was very angry, and screamed with rage; but she could not come within two yards of him, for the flower he held in his hand was his safeguard. He looked around at the birds in the cages, but there were many, many nightingales, and how then should he find out which one was his Jorinda?

While he was thinking what to do, he saw the fairy had taken down one of the cages, and was making her way off through the door. He ran after her, touched the cage with the flower, and Jorinda stood before him, and threw her arms round his neck looking as beautiful as ever, as beautiful as when they walked together in the wood.

Then he touched all the other birds with the flower, so that they all took their old forms again. And he took Jorinda home, where they were married, and lived happily together many years: and so did a good many other lads, whose maidens had been forced to sing in the old fairy's cages by themselves, much longer than they liked.

Jack the Giant-Killer

From Andrew Lang's *Blue Fairy Book*

IN THE REIGN of the famous King Arthur there lived in Cornwall a lad named Jack, who was a boy of a bold temper. He took delight in hearing or reading of conjurers, giants and fairies; and used to listen eagerly to the deeds of the knights of King Arthur's Round Table.

In those days there lived on St Michael's Mount, off Cornwall, a huge giant, eighteen metres high and nine metres round; his fierce and savage looks were the terror of all who beheld him.

He dwelled in a gloomy cavern on the top of the

mountain, and used to wade over to the mainland in search of prey. He would throw half a dozen oxen upon his back, and tie three times as many sheep and hogs round his waist, and march back to his abode.

The giant had done this for many years when Jack resolved to destroy him. Jack took a horn, a shovel, a pickaxe, his armour and a dark lantern, and one winter's evening he went to the mount. There he dug a pit twenty-two metres deep and twenty broad. He covered the top over so as to make it look like solid ground. He then blew his horn so loudly that the giant awoke and came out of his den crying out: "You villain! You shall pay for this! I'll broil you for my breakfast!" He had just finished, when, taking one step further, he tumbled into the pit, and Jack struck him a blow on the head with his pickaxe which killed him. Jack then returned home to cheer his friends with the news.

Another giant, called Blunderbore, vowed to be revenged on Jack if ever he should have him in his power. This giant lived in an enchanted castle in a lonely wood and one day came across Jack lying under a tree in the wood, asleep. The giant carried Jack off to his castle, where he locked him up in a large room, the floor of which was covered with the bodies, skulls and bones of men and women.

Soon afterwards the giant went to fetch his brother, to take a meal off his flesh. Jack saw with terror through the bars of his prison the two giants approaching. Then he noticed in one corner of the room a strong rope. He took courage and, making a slip-knot at each end, threw them over their heads, and tied it to the window-bars; then he pulled till he had choked them. When they were dead, he slid down the rope and stabbed them in their hearts.

Jack next took a great bunch of keys from the pocket of Blunderbore, and went into the castle again. He searched through all the rooms, and in one of them found three ladies tied up by the hair and almost starved to death. They told him that their husbands had been killed by the giants, who had then condemned them to be starved to death because they would not eat the flesh of their own dead husbands.

"Ladies," said Jack, "I have put an end to the monster and his wicked brother; and I give you this castle and all the riches it contains, to make some amends for the dreadful pains you have felt." He then very politely gave them the keys of the castle.

Having hitherto been successful in all his undertakings, Jack resolved not to be idle in future; he therefore furnished himself with a horse, a cap of knowledge, a sword of sharpness, shoes of swiftness and an invisible coat, the better to perform the wonderful enterprises that lay before him.

He travelled over hills and dales till, arriving at the foot of a high mountain, he knocked at the door of a lonely house. An old man let him in, and when Jack was seated, the old man said: "My son, on the top of this mountain is an enchanted castle, kept by the giant Galligantus and a vile magician. They seized a duke's daughter, as she was walking in her father's garden, and then they brought her here transformed into a deer."

Jack promised that in the morning, at the risk of his life, he would break the enchantment; and after a sound sleep he rose early, put on his invisible coat, and got ready for the attempt.

When he had climbed to the top of the mountain he saw two fiery griffins, but he passed between them without the least fear of danger, for they could not see him because of his invisible coat. On the castle gate he found a golden trumpet, under which were written these lines:

> Whoever can this trumpet blow
> Shall cause the giant's overthrow.

As soon as Jack had read this he seized the trumpet and blew a shrill blast, which made the gates fly open

and the very castle itself tremble.

The giant and the magician now knew that their wicked course was at an end, and they stood biting their thumbs and shaking with fear. Jack, with his sword of sharpness, soon killed the giant, and the magician was then carried away by a whirlwind; and every knight and beautiful lady who had been changed into birds and beasts returned to their proper shapes. The castle vanished away like smoke, and the head of the giant Galligantus was then sent to King Arthur.

The knights and ladies rested that night at the old man's house, and next day they set out for the Court. Jack's fame had now spread through the whole country, and the duke gave him his daughter in marriage. After this the king gave him a large estate, on which he and his lady lived the rest of their days in joy and contentment.

Tamlane

From *More English Fairy Tales,*
by Joseph Jacobs

YOUNG TAMLANE was son of Earl Murray, and Burd Janet was daughter of Dunbar, Earl of March. And when they were young they loved one another and plighted their troth. But when the time came near for their marrying, Tamlane disappeared, and none knew what had become of him.

Many, many days after he had disappeared, Burd Janet was wandering in Carterhaugh Wood, though she had been warned not to go there. She came to a bush of broom and began plucking it. She had not taken more than three flowers when by her side up started young Tamlane.

"Where come ye from, Tamlane?" Burd Janet said. "And why have you been away so long?"

"From Elfland I come," said young Tamlane. "The Queen of Elfland has made me her knight."

"But how did you get there?" asked Burd Janet.

"I was hunting one day, and as I rode widershins round yon hill, a deep drowsiness fell upon me, and when I awoke, behold! I was in Elfland."

"Oh, tell me if aught I can do will save you?"

"Tomorrow night is Hallowe'en, and the fairy court will then ride through England and Scotland, and if you would rescue me from Elfland you must stand by Miles Cross between twelve and one o' the night, and cast holy water all around you."

"But how shall I know you, Tamlane," cried Burd Janet, "amid so many knights I've ne'er seen before?"

"The first court of elves that come by let pass. The next court you shall curtsey to, but do naught nor say aught. But the third court that comes by is the chief court, and at the head rides the Queen of Elfland.

And I shall ride by her side upon a milk-white steed with a star in my crown. Watch my hands, Janet, the right one will be gloved but the left one will be bare, and by that token you will know me."

"But how to save you?" asked Burd Janet.

"You must spring upon me suddenly, and I will fall to the ground. Then seize me quick, and whatever change befall me, for they will exercise all their magic on me, cling on till they turn me into red-hot iron. Then cast me into the water and I will be turned back into a man. Cast then your green mantle over me, and I shall be yours, and be of the world again."

So Burd Janet promised to do all for Tamlane, and the next night at midnight she took her stand by Miles Cross and cast holy water all around her.

Soon there came riding by the Elfin Court, first over the mound went a troop on black steeds, and then another troop on brown. But in the third court, all on milk-white steeds, she saw the Queen of

Elfland, and by her side a knight with a star in his crown, with his right hand gloved and the left bare. Then she knew this was Tamlane, and springing forward she seized the bridle of the milk-white steed and pulled its rider down. As soon as he had touched the ground she let go of the bridle and seized Tamlane in her arms.

"He's won, he's won amongst us all," shrieked out the eldritch crew, and all came around her and tried their spells on young Tamlane.

First they turned him in Janet's arms like frozen ice, then into a huge flame of roaring fire. Then, again, the fire vanished and an adder was skipping through her arms, but still she held on; and then they turned him into a snake that reared up as if to bite her, and yet she held on. Then suddenly a dove was struggling in her arms, and almost flew away. Then they turned him into a swan, but all was in vain, till at last he was turned into red-hot iron, and this she cast into a well of water and then he turned back into a man. She quickly cast her green mantle over him, and young Tamlane was Burd Janet's. And the Elfin Court rode away, and Burd Janet and young Tamlane went their way homewards and were married soon afterwards.

The Twelve Brothers

Retold by Andrew Lang in his *Red Fairy Book*,
after the Brothers Grimm

THERE WERE ONCE UPON A TIME a king and a queen who had twelve children, all of whom were boys. One day the king said to his wife: "If our thirteenth child is a girl, all her twelve brothers must die, so that the kingdom may be hers alone."

Then he ordered twelve coffins to be made, and put these away in an empty room and, giving the key to his wife, he bade her tell no one of it.

The queen grieved and refused to be comforted, so much so that the youngest boy, who was always with her, and whom she had christened Benjamin, left her

no peace, till she went and unlocked the room and
showed him the twelve little coffins and explained.
She wept bitterly, but her son comforted her and said:
"Don't cry, dear Mother; we'll escape somehow."

"Yes," replied his mother, "that is what you must
do – go with your eleven brothers out into the wood.
Let one of you always sit on the highest tree you can
find, keeping watch on the tower of the castle. If I
give birth to a little son I will wave a white flag, and
then you may safely return; but if I give birth to a
little daughter I will wave a red flag, which will warn
you to fly away as quickly as you can. Every night I
will get up and pray for you."

Then she blessed her sons and they set out into the

wood. They found a very high oak tree, and there they sat, turn about, keeping their eyes always fixed on the castle tower. On the twelfth day, when the turn came to Benjamin, he noticed a flag waving in the air, but alas! It was not white, but blood red, the sign which told them they must all die. When the brothers heard this they were very angry, and said: "Shall we suffer death for the sake of a wretched girl? Let us vow that wherever and whenever we shall meet one of her sex, she shall die at our hands."

Then they went their way deeper into the wood, and in the middle of it, where it was thickest and darkest, they came upon a little enchanted house which stood empty.

"Here," they said, "let us take up our abode, and you, Benjamin, you shall stay at home and keep house for us; we will go out and fetch food." So they went forth into the wood and foraged and hunted. They lived for ten years in this little house, and the time slipped merrily away.

Meantime, their little sister grew up kind-hearted

and of a fair countenance, with a gold star right in the middle of her forehead. One day the girl looked down from her window and saw twelve men's shirts hanging on the washing line to dry, and asked her mother: "Who do these shirts belong to? Surely they are far too small for my father?"

And the queen answered sadly: "Dear child, they belong to your twelve brothers."

"But where are my twelve brothers?" said the girl. "I have never even heard of them."

"Heaven alone knows!" replied her mother. Then she took the girl and opened the locked-up room and showed her the twelve coffins.

The queen told all that had happened, and when she had finished her daughter said: "Do not cry, dearest Mother; I will go and seek my brothers till I find them." So she took the twelve shirts and went on straight into the middle of the big wood. She walked all day long, and came in the evening to the little enchanted house. She stepped in and found a youth who, marvelling at her beauty, at the royal robes she wore, and at the golden star on her forehead, asked her where she came from and whither she was going.

"I am a princess," she answered, "and am seeking for my twelve brothers. I mean to wander as far as the blue sky stretches over the earth till I find them."

Then she showed him the twelve shirts which she had taken with her, and Benjamin saw that it must be his sister, and said: "I am your youngest brother."

So they wept for joy, and hugged each other.

After a time Benjamin said: "Dear sister, there is still a problem, for we had all agreed that any girl we met should die at our hands, because it was for the sake of a girl that we had to leave our kingdom. Go and hide under that tub till our eleven brothers come in, and I'll make matters right with them."

She did as she was bid, and soon the others came home from the chase and sat down to supper.

"Well, well," Benjamin said to his brothers, "you've been out in the wood all the day and I've stayed quietly at home, and yet I've got exciting news!"

"Then tell us," they cried.

But he answered: "Only on condition that you promise faithfully that the first girl we meet shall not be killed."

"She shall be spared," they promised, "only tell us the news."

Then Benjamin said: "Our sister is here!" and he lifted up the tub and the princess stepped forward, looking so lovely and sweet and charming that they all loved her on the spot.

They arranged that she should stay at home with Benjamin and help him in the housework, while the rest of the brothers went out into the wood to forage and hunt. The princess made herself so generally useful that her brothers were delighted, and they all lived happily together.

One day the two at home prepared a fine feast, and when they were all assembled they sat down and ate and drank and made merry. Now there was a little garden round the enchanted house, in which grew twelve tall lilies. The girl, wishing to please her brothers, started to pluck the twelve flowers, meaning

to present one to each of them after supper. But hardly had she begun when her brothers were turned into twelve ravens, who flew croaking over the wood, and the house and garden vanished also.

So the poor girl found herself left all alone in the wood, and as she looked round her she noticed an old woman standing close by, who said: "My child, what

have you done? Why didn't you leave the flowers alone? Now your brothers are changed for ever into ravens."

The girl asked, sobbing: "Is there no means of setting them free?"

"There is only one way," said the old woman, "and that is so difficult that you won't free them by it, for you would have to be dumb and not laugh for seven years."

The girl said to herself: "If that is all, I am quite sure I can free my brothers." So she searched for a high tree, and climbed up it and spun all day long, never laughing nor speaking one word.

Now it happened one day that a king who was out hunting had a greyhound, who ran sniffing to the tree on which the girl sat. When the king looked up and beheld the beautiful princess, he was so enchanted that he asked her to be his wife. She gave no answer, but nodded slightly. Then he climbed up the tree, lifted her down, and bore her home to his palace. Their marriage was celebrated with much ceremony, but the bride neither spoke nor laughed.

When they had lived a few years happily together, the king's mother, who was a wicked woman, began to speak ill of the young queen, accusing her of many evil things. The queen could not speak for herself to protest, and eventually the king let himself be talked over, and condemned his wife to death.

So a great fire was lit in the courtyard of the palace, where she was to be burned, and the king watched from an upper window, crying bitterly, for he still loved his wife dearly. But just as she had been bound to the stake, and the flames were licking her garments, the very last moment of the seven years came. Then a sudden rushing sound was heard and twelve ravens swooped downwards. As soon as they touched the ground they turned into her twelve brothers, and she knew that she had freed them.

They quenched the flames and, unbinding their dear sister from the stake, they kissed and hugged her again and again. And now that she was able to speak, she told the king why she had been dumb and not able to laugh.

The king rejoiced greatly when he heard she was innocent, and they all lived happily ever after.